SAFARI TALES

SAFARI TALES

SAFARI TALES

By
Mary Weeks Millard

Illustrated by Catherine L Owen

ISBN-13: 978 1 914273 05 6

Copyright © 2021 by John Ritchie Ltd.
40 Beansburn, Kilmarnock, Scotland

www.ritchiechristianmedia.co.uk

Typeset by John Ritchie Ltd., Kilmarnock
Printed by Bell & Bain Ltd., Glasgow

Dedication

To Abby and Aaron, my Rwandan adopted grandchildren.
From Jaaja Mariya with love.

Acknowledgements

My grateful thanks to Catherine (Cat) for her amazing illustrations for this book. I know it took you many hours to draw them.

My thanks to all the team at John Ritchie who have been so helpful in producing and promoting his book.

My thanks to my ever-patient husband, Malcolm, who constantly encourages me as I write.

INTRODUCTION

This is to tell you how my monkey puppet, Safari, joined my family, and how this book of stories began.

A long time ago, before I became a very old grandmother, I used to work as a nurse in a doctors' surgery in England. There were five doctors and four nurses and many other people who helped in the surgery, so that sick people were helped to get well, and well people helped so that they didn't get sick. We were always very busy – often so busy that we didn't get a lot of time to go shopping. One day a lady came to the surgery – not because she was sick, but because she was selling books and thought that the busy staff might like to browse through them in their coffee breaks, and perhaps buy one or two.

The books were put into a box and left in the staff room in the basement of the building. In the box, along with the books, was a monkey puppet. Someone must have looked at him one day, and not put him back into his bag very tidily, because there he was, his head poking out of the bag, getting dusty and dirty as the days went by. He was in a place that no self-respecting monkey should have been! At the very least he should have been on the shelf of a toy shop where people could see and admire him!

When I went to have my tea or coffee breaks I kept seeing this monkey peeping out of his bag and looking at me – he looked so sad all on his own with no-one to love or take care of him and after a few weeks I couldn't bear it any more – I just *had* to buy him and take him home.

At that time all my own children were grown up and I only had one granddaughter, who lived a very long way away and I wasn't often able to see her – so it seemed silly at the time to buy the monkey but I did anyway. The puppet had a twinkle in his eye which made me love him - so I paid the money and took him home.

I found a soft brush and cleaned off the dust and dirt which had collected on the hat and jacket he was wearing, and then decided that, as he was joining the family, he must have a name. I called him 'Safari' – because he had a very smart safari set of clothes. He no longer lived in a bag with just his face poking out but sat in a chair in the hallway of our house. He could see everyone who came in and out of the house and they could give him a smile, or even a hug if they liked.

He soon became a very useful monkey. From time to time I went to a country in the middle of Africa – a very special country called Rwanda, and I took Safari with me. He helped me a lot when I wanted to teach children about Jesus and how much He loves them. Since then Safari has come on real safari adventures with me and has now travelled to several countries in Africa.

Safari was left in a dark, dirty place – like rubbish, just pushed into a bag, and no-one seemed to want him. It was not the right place for a lovely, smart toy monkey.

In the same way, very sadly, sometimes people, even children, can feel as if they are in a dark and lonely place and no-one wants them – not in the right place at all. God wants us all to come home and be in His family – that's why He sent Jesus to earth, so that He could die for us and make the way for us to come into God's family. He forgives us for all the wrong things we have done and makes us clean again. He gives us a new name and wants us to tell other people about His love and His story – just like Safari helps me. So, I hope you enjoy these stories about a real monkey called Safari and learn more about Jesus, too.

SAFARI EXPLORES THE BIG BEYOND

Safari was always a restless monkey – he just loved adventures! His mum often gave a big sigh when she heard him say, "Mum I'm bored! What can I do now?" She wished he was more like the other small monkeys in the forest, content to play around the trees, swinging from branch to branch, eating sweet bananas, but never going far from the nest of leaves where they lived, high up in the trees.

Every day Safari thought to himself, "Where can I go today? – I want to explore the *Big Beyond* and find out about the world beyond our nest and this bit of the forest."

One morning he decided he would do just that! He began to jabber and squeak, which is what monkeys do when they are excited - then he put on his lovely jacket and hat which always made him feel important and like a real explorer, and he scampered down the tree where the nest was, onto the trail through the forest. Soon he had scampered up another tree and began swinging through the trees down to the river. Real explorers went to rivers and mountains as well as forests, and they explored the *Big Beyond* – the world outside of his cosy nest and the trees around it.

He stopped at a banana palm and pulled off a couple of sweet bananas to give himself some energy, then continued his journey. Eventually he reached the riverbank. By now his little arms were aching, because Safari was only a small monkey – but he knew there was 'no gain without pain' and was determined not to think about his sore arms, but just about being a famous monkey explorer of the *Big Beyond*.

He climbed down from the branches of the tree and peered into the river. It was green and looked scary – and to his great surprise he saw another monkey who also had a jacket and hat just like his, who was in the water! Now forest monkeys don't much like water, so he was very surprised to see it there. Wasn't it scared of the crocodiles?

Safari looked again at the monkey in the river and scratched his head (as monkeys do when they are thinking) – wondering why the jacket didn't look wet. He saw the monkey in the river was scratching his head, too – which he thought was funny. So, he jabbered to him, and waved. The monkey was waving back.

Then he decided to get on with his exploring and walked a little further down the river – only to find that the monkey seemed to be floating down the river, too. It was all too strange for Safari, so he thought that he would put his back paw into the water. Ugh! It was so cold and like many monkeys, he hated water and couldn't swim. The strange little monkey in the river pulled a face, too - but he still seemed quite happy in the water. Safari scratched his head again to think of this big wonder he had discovered on his adventure in the *Big Beyond* – and the monkey in the water did the same. Then suddenly Safari found himself slipping down the riverbank and was almost in the water when he felt a big tight 'thing' come around his middle and pull him out. It was Tembo the elephant who, using his trunk, whirled him up into the air and placed him firmly on the ground far from the river.

"You silly little monkey-child," he said in his deep elephant voice. "If you had fallen into the water you would have drowned or been eaten by the crocodile."

"But," stuttered Safari, "there was a little monkey just like me in the water and he was ok. He wasn't even wet!"

"Oh, little monkey-child – that wasn't another monkey – that was just your reflection in the water."

"What's a reflection?" asked Safari, and Tembo explained to him what it was – just the river showing a picture of him.

When he understood, Safari realised that he had truly been in danger of falling into the river and the elephant had saved his life. "Thank you," he said, and went home a wiser little monkey.

Jesus can save us, too, from all the dangers of sin and Satan as he tries to harm us – we need to ask Him to forgive us for the silly things and wrong things we do, and to teach us His good way of living.

SAFARI GETS LOST

Safari was very excited! All the monkey family were going out for the day. It was the hottest and driest season of the year and there wasn't a lot of fruit around to eat – and fruit was the favourite food of the monkeys, so they had a good idea. They would go on a banana hunt.

That sounds fun, doesn't it? Safari thought so, too. He made sure he put on his hat which shaded his eyes from the strong sunlight, and he wore his smart jacket and was soon jabbering away to his mum.

"When are we leaving? Do hurry up, I'm ready to go."

His mum was saying things to him like, "Just settle down and be patient – it won't be long" and "Be sensible when we all start off and don't wander away from the clan," and even more importantly, "Don't stop and talk to strangers."

Safari hardly heard what she was saying and didn't take any notice because she was always saying things like that.

Eventually they left their monkey nest, which was made of leaves and high in a tree. They scampered down to the ground and met all their friends in a nearby clearing. You should have heard the noise when all the monkeys got together! It scared the birds out of the trees, the deer out of the grass and even the tall giraffe was not impressed.

So, everyone set off looking for bananas. They went to a nearby plantation, and although there were plenty of banana trees, they found very, very few bananas. Still, it was fun for the monkey children playing hide and seek among the trees. After a while they became a bit bored with trailing after the adults and just looking for bananas, so they began to make a ball. They collected some dry leaves and some long vine stems and made the leaves into a ball shape and wound the vines around to help them keep their shape. The ball grew bigger and bigger. Then the monkey children began to look for a clearing where they could play football.

There were ten monkey children, so it was great - they could play five-a-side. The little monkeys were so caught up in their game that they forgot they were supposed to stay near their parents and forgot all about the fact they were supposed to be hunting bananas, and they didn't realise that their parents had gone on ahead of them.

Meanwhile, their parents had found a place where there were some very good banana palms which had lovely small, sweet finger bananas. They began to feast on them, but after a few minutes Safari's mum realized that she hadn't seen her son for a little while. She guessed that he was probably with his friends and their parents, but whenever food was around, Safari was usually the first to be seen eating! She stopped eating and looked around, only to see that the other parents were also looking around, but there were no children to be seen!

Then they began to be worried. Where were their children? They decided they would have to go back down the trail to see if they could find them. They looked here and there. They stopped and asked a giraffe, because with his long neck he could see further than they could.

The giraffe looked around, stretching his long neck as far as he could.

"They are over by the water hole," he told them.

This made the parents even more worried. The water hole was a dangerous place, especially for young animals and small ones like monkeys. It was full of crocodiles who were fierce. Crocodiles would just love a little monkey for lunch, and a hippopotamus could easily trample one underfoot.

They rushed down and there were their children, happily playing footie, oblivious to all the dangers around them and not realising that their mothers were sick with worry.

The mummy monkeys started to scold, jabbering away; "I told you not to wander off," "I told you not to leave my side!" "You are such a naughty monkey" they were saying. "We thought we had lost you – look how near you are to this dangerous place – the water hole!"

The little monkeys looked surprised. "Sorry," some of them muttered. "We were just playing," said Safari. "We had no idea how near we were to the water hole or how quickly the time had gone."

"I'm so hungry," moaned one little monkey, tears beginning to roll down his face.

The mummy monkeys took them and swung them up onto their backs and led them back through the jungle trail to the plantation where the rest of the clan were still eating the sweet bananas.

By now the parents were calming down and not so cross because their children were safe, but they had been very scared for their safety, and thought they might have lost them for ever.

For the rest of the day, Safari was very quiet and stayed close to his mum. He had learnt a big lesson – it was important to stay near to his mum and listen to what she told him, because when he went off on his own, he was in danger.

Now that is true for us as Christians. We need to listen to Jesus and take note of what He says, and stay close to Him every day, because we, too, are in great danger when we go off on our own and think we know better. Jesus loves us so much He wants to protect us from the evil and dangers in the world.

SAFARI MAKES UP STORIES

Safari was sitting on a branch of a big tree with a couple of his best friends. You should hear them squeaking away as they chatted together. Safari was telling them about an adventure he had.

"I was walking along the path by the river, doing nothing special, when suddenly I heard a hiss. There, right in front of me was a cobra, a huge spitting cobra! He raised his head and looked at me with his beady eyes. He thought I was scared. I was a bit, but I didn't show it. Before he could spit at me, I jumped behind a rock, picked up a stone and threw it at him. It hit him on the head so that he died."

The other monkeys looked at him in amazement.

"You never did! You are telling stories," one of his friends said.

"You couldn't have killed a cobra," the other declared.

"Oh, I did," lied Safari. "I am the bravest little monkey in the forest!"

His monkey friends looked at him with admiration, and it made Safari feel so good that he almost believed his own story.

"I really am the bravest little monkey in the whole forest," he thought to himself.

Another day, Safari was swinging in the trees with some other little monkey friends. They were telling each other to be careful near the clearing where there were no trees, because a pack of hyenas had been on the prowl.

Once again, Safari began to tell a boastful story.

"You know," he said, "I once met a hyena. He was a big, nasty male dog. I was all on my own and he looked at me with two mean eyes and growled. I decided I would not be afraid and would stare him out. I stared and stared and stared! In the end he slunk away with his tail between his legs. I am the bravest little monkey in the whole forest!"

Safari's little monkey friends looked at him in disbelief.

"You are telling us lies," they told him. "What you say cannot be true."

"Oh yes, it is, cross my heart and hope to die," lied Safari.

Once again, his friends believed him and looked at him with great admiration and amazement.

It did make Safari feel ten feet tall and his chest swelled out with pride, for he almost believed his own stories. In fact, he was sure he was the bravest little monkey not just in the whole forest, but in the whole wide world!

So, Safari began to get into a very bad habit. It was like sliding down a slippery slope – once he had started, he couldn't stop and began to make up more and more untrue stories and boasted about himself to his friends. His friends no longer believed him, but just pretended to listen. When he had left them, and they were on their own they laughed about him among themselves.

Safari, however, was sure he was THE MOST SPECIAL MONKEY in the whole world!

However, there came a day – a terrible day, when he learnt that telling lies is bad, and telling the truth is what matters.

It happened on a cold, wet morning. The rain was dripping from every leaf on every tree, and each time he swung on a branch, the rain dripped down his fur. However, he told himself that he was the bravest little monkey in the world so he would be quite safe going down to the river and he would see what adventures he could find.

It was very slippery down by the river and the noise of the waterfall was deafening. In fact, even the noise made him a bit frightened. It was swollen by so much rain. For a moment he stopped to think how terrible it would be if he fell in, but then he reminded himself that such a clever monkey as he would never do such a silly thing.

He was looking at the river and began to admire his own reflection in the water. He was so full of good thoughts about himself that he didn't see the way the movement of the water had changed or hear the very quiet 'swish, swish' noise.

A very large crocodile was slithering out of the water and up the bank towards him. Suddenly, Safari saw him. The crocodile was watching him through his beady eyes, looking with delight at the good meal in front of him. He was showing the row of sharp teeth and the terrified little monkey was frozen with fear. He opened his mouth to scream and at first no noise came out, but eventually he managed to scream,

"Help me! Help me! there is a crocodile who wants to eat me!"

Some of his friends who were in the nearby trees looked down and shrugged their shoulders.

"It's just that silly monkey telling his stories, don't worry about him," they said. They called out to Safari, "You, the bravest little monkey in the forest, you need not worry," as they ran off.

The crocodile was now right out of the river and getting ever closer to Safari. He was so scared that he just couldn't move - his legs and arms felt like jelly and he felt sick.

He realised how silly he'd been. He wasn't even the tiniest bit brave. He was just an ordinary little monkey who was about to become a crocodile's dinner!

In despair, a tear rolled down his cheek, then another, and then a whole flood of them! If he hadn't told all those lies, then perhaps he wouldn't be trapped now.

He was sure his end had come when a big hand reached down and pulled him away, just as the crocodile jaws had opened to snap him up and eat him. It was Safari's father! He quickly pulled him up and swung away into the trees to safety.

Safari was still crying and shaking all over and his daddy just held him close until he was calm, and he realized he was now safe. Then his daddy explained, "I heard some of your friends saying you were calling for help, but they thought it was just one of your made-up stories. I thought so, too, but since you are my son I had to come and be sure – and how glad I am that I did!"

"Oh Daddy," sobbed Safari, "what a stupid monkey I have been. I told so many lies that I really believed that I was the bravest little monkey in the whole forest, even in the whole world! I am sorry for all the lies. Thank you so much for coming and saving me."

When they were safely back at home in their nest, Daddy talked to him.

"Safari, you have learnt today that telling lies leads you into a trap which can destroy you. Learn something else, too. You are special just because you are Safari and my son. You don't have to make up stories to make yourself into someone who you are not and were never meant to be. Always tell the truth then people will believe and respect you. That way you will grow up to be brave, for it takes courage to tell the truth.

Our enemy, Satan, is called the father of lies and he wants us to get caught in a trap of lies. But we need to follow Jesus, who is the way, the truth and the life. We can ask Him to help us to have courage and become people who can always be trusted.

SAFARI LEARNS A LESSON

One day Safari woke up with a headache and was in a bad mood. He crawled out of the nest of leaves and his young brother came running up to him.

"Come and play with me," he said.

Safari pushed him away roughly, almost pushing him over.

"Go away," he said, "I don't want to play with a silly baby like you!"

He turned away from his little brother without noticing that his eyes were beginning to fill up with tears.

Safari swung from tree to tree until he reached the river. Although the forest monkeys do not really like the water, Safari had got used to the river and found it cool and refreshing to play near its banks. He was always very careful to watch out for crocodiles after his nasty experience when he was almost eaten up by one and so did not get too near the edge and fall in the river.

This morning, because he was cross, had a headache and felt sorry that he had been mean to his brother, he kicked every stone and clump of grass as he scampered along the path by the river.

Safari kicked one big stone and a frog jumped out at him. It was a large, green slimy frog. Safari was startled. For a few seconds the monkey and the frog just looked at each other.

"You scared me, you horrible green, slimy frog," shouted Safari, unkindly.

"You scared me, too – kicking my stone like that," answered the frog. "Just because I am a frog and smaller than you, you don't have to be rude to me."

"Yes, I do," replied Safari, "I *hate* frogs and toads – you are horrible creatures and I *am* much bigger and better than you. I think I will catch you and kill you and make this river a better place without you," he said crossly.

The frog looked at him for a moment. "Be careful little monkey," he said, "all the animals here are God's creatures." With a big jump he leaped away from Safari. Safari tried to catch him, but the frog was far too quick for him and was soon happily swimming in the river.

"Huh," shouted Safari, "you be careful slimy frog. I will catch you one day!" He went on his way crosser than ever.

He walked along the river bank a bit further and after a while his headache seemed a little better. Safari began to hum a tune as he walked along, but suddenly he stopped in his tracks. A very large creature was blocking his path, standing in his way. It was black and white with horns and a loud 'moo' came out of its mouth.

Safari wasn't used to seeing cows as they didn't live in the forest, but this one had become thirsty and decided to have a drink in the river. Safari felt quite frightened at the sight of the big creature blocking his path and decided he had better be polite to this large animal.

"Good morning," he said to the cow, but the cow just mooed loudly at him.

"Get out of my way," it said. "Be careful, my hoof could crush you. After all I am a cow - a very important and expensive creature. Everyone honours me because I give milk to the humans."

Safari was quite frightened of this big and important creature, but he remembered what the frog had said to him and repeated the words, - "You be careful Mrs Cow, for all the animals here are God's creatures."

The cow turned her head and stared at the small monkey, then opened her mouth and bellowed such a loud 'moo' that Safari grabbed a branch of a tree and started to swing and didn't stop until he got home.

His father was waiting for him when he arrived. Safari could see by his face that he was in trouble – Daddy was angry.

"Come here Safari," he told him, "we need to talk."

"Yes, Daddy," he answered, and his father picked him up.

"There is something you need to learn about today," his Daddy told him, "because you were very unkind to your little brother this morning. Do you think that you are better than him just because you are bigger?"

"No," said Safari in a little voice.

"Do you think I am better because I am older than you?" Daddy asked him.

"Yes," was Safari's answer.

"Well, you have a big lesson to learn – and that is that we are all equal and very precious in God, our Maker's eyes.

Every creature is precious, whether big or small, young or old, whatever they look like and wherever they have come from, whether they are wise or whether they are silly.

The rule of our family is that we love one another and all the creatures around us in the forest."

"Yes, Daddy," said Safari who was feeling very sad that he'd been horrible to his brother. "I'll try to learn this lesson. I'm sorry I was horrible to my brother – please forgive me."

"You need to go to him and say sorry and ask him to forgive you" was Daddy's reply. "Don't be proud because you are older and bigger than he is and maybe you know a bit more than he does."

Safari thought of how mean he was to the frog as well as to his brother and was ashamed. Then he remembered how the big cow had looked down on him and how frightened he had felt. He realised that it would be much better if they all loved and respected each other.

This is a big lesson we all need to learn – we must love each other, no matter if we look different, if we are younger or older – we should love and respect everyone and everything God has made, people and creatures and the beautiful world around us.

SAFARI'S SATURDAY

It was Saturday. Safari's mum got up with a big sigh. There was so much to do on a Saturday – and she was already tired. Safari's dad had gone out and was swinging through the branches of the trees, foraging food for the family. Life in the forest wasn't always easy, especially at certain times of the year when food was scarce.

Mum looked around the nest and gave another big sigh. They loved the tree in which they lived, but it did get into such a mess with Mum, Dad, Safari and his little brother Tutu. It did need cleaning out! It needed fresh banana leaves to give it a good strong lining to make it into a good nest again. However, Mum needed first to go to the plantation and it was a long way, especially swinging through the trees with a baby on her back.

Safari woke up and was excited. He *loved* Saturdays! He jabbered and squeaked – which is what monkeys do when they are excited. He couldn't wait to go out to the clearing and meet up with his mates. He looked at his mum – she seemed a bit cross and grumpy and looked tired. He thought it would be a good idea to keep out of her way, and that suited him very well as he wanted to go and play football. He just loved playing football. "Maybe I'll score a goal today," he thought to himself, getting excited at the very thought of his mates cheering as the ball landed in the net! It was only a fun match, but it mattered very much to Safari that he played well. Yes, Safari *loved* Saturdays – a whole day just to please himself.

He snatched a couple of bananas, the last couple he could see in the nest, and ate them greedily, dropping the skins on the banana leaf floor without even thinking that he was making more work for his mum. He saw his mum swing baby Tutu onto her back and called out, 'Love you Mum' as he began to run down the tree trunk.

"But Safari ..." Mum started to say, "could you ...?" However, Safari ran off before he could hear any more. He knew she wanted him to do something for her, but he wanted to play football with his mates.

He arrived at the clearing, which was a nice patch of level ground, with some grass where sometimes human children played as well as the young monkeys. Lots of his friends were there waiting to play.

"Yay! you're here," one of his friends greeted him. "We were waiting for you."

Soon the teams had been chosen and the game started. Safari found it hard to concentrate even though he had been looking forward to playing. All he could think about was running away from the nest saying, "Love you Mum," just when she was trying to ask him to do something. He felt bad inside about that – if he really loved his mum he would have stopped and listened and done as she asked.

After a while of kicking the ball around he knew he wasn't playing very well. He wouldn't score goals today - he just wasn't in the right mood anymore. Nothing felt right inside.

He decided he should go home, forget about football and see if he could help his mum. It wasn't easy to make that choice, but even though he loved football, he knew that he loved his mum even more.

"Sorry, mates," he said, "I have to go now."

"What? Where are you going?" one of them asked. He knew that they would laugh at him, but he told them anyway. "I'm going home. My mum needs me to help her," he told them as he ran off the pitch and back into the forest, hearing his friends laughing in the distance.

When he got home, he found his mum was nowhere to be seen. "I can still help," he thought to himself, as he set to work and dragged all the dirty leaves, banana skins and other debris out of the nest and down the tree trunk. It was smelly work cleaning up all the mess. Then he went off into the forest to collect new leaves to make it fresh and clean. Safari was surprised that he was happy doing something to help his mum as a surprise, and he hummed a tune to himself as he worked. He forgot all about playing football. When the nest was remade, he went off into the forest to find some nuts to put into the store, and he filled the store right to the very top. He hadn't realised before what fun it could be when he helped someone else.

Safari was squeaking away so happily that he didn't hear his mum come wearily home, dragging a large bunch of bananas behind her, with Tutu still on her back. It was her squeak of joy that made him jump and he realised she was home. That happy squeak from his mum was worth all his hard work, better than all the cheers of his mates on the football pitch when he scored a goal!

"Thank you so much Safari," she said. "You gave up your football match to come home and help me, and I needed help so badly today."

"But I love you, Mum, I really do," answered Safari, giving her a big hug, and helping Tutu climb off her back. "Now you can go and rest ... You look so tired."

Safari thought it was the best Saturday he had ever had, and it certainly was the best that his mum had known for a long time.

This story reminds me that Jesus tells us to love one another, and although that may not always be easy, it brings happiness to Him, to others and to us. We all want JOY in our lives and one way to find that is to put Jesus first, Others next, Yourself last.

NEW NEIGHBOURS

One day Safari and Tutu were playing together at the bottom of the tree which was their home. Tutu was growing quickly and now didn't need to be carried by his mother all the time, and Safari was teaching him how to kick a ball. He'd made the ball himself by scrunching some strong leaves into a ball shape and then tying them there with the long dry stem of a vine. It worked very well, especially for a little monkey like Tutu, who didn't kick too hard. For the football matches with his friends, the boys made much larger and stronger balls, but used the same method.

As they were playing, they heard a bit of a commotion in a nearby tree. Someone was jabbering away in a monkey language, but strangely, it was not the same as Safari and all their friends and family spoke, and he couldn't understand the words. He took Tutu's hand and they walked nearer the tree and saw that some strange monkeys were there and seemed to be busy building a nest. The monkeys were standing up on their hind legs and stared at the two little brown monkeys who had come over. The new monkeys had black and white faces and looked a bit scary, so Safari and Tutu rushed back to their tree and scampered up into the nest.

"There are strange monkey animals making a nest nearby – we were scared, so we ran away," said Safari to his mother, who was tidying up the banana skins on the floor.

"What do you mean – how are they strange?" asked his mum.

"They stand on their hind legs and stare and are black, but with black and white faces – not a bit like us," he told her. "I couldn't understand what they were saying, either."

"Well, I have never seen monkeys like that, but I am sure we will soon make friends," she replied, "but you were right to come home. I've always told you not to talk to strangers."

When Dad came home, he heard all about the new neighbours. Safari and Tutu were very excited and told him all they knew.

"I'll go and welcome them to the neighbourhood," he said, "after I have eaten".

Safari and Tutu were jumping up and down and swinging on the branches with excitement when their father went off to visit the new neighbours. It seemed a long time before he came back.

"It was hard for us to understand each other," he explained, "for these are mountain monkeys who have travelled all the way from the east of the country. They speak our language, but it sounds very different. I had to be patient and listen carefully to them and they had the same problem with me. The weather has been unkind to them in the mountains and there is no food, so they have been travelling north and west for many days to find somewhere to live. They have a boy your age, Safari, and a baby girl who is still carried and fed by her mother. They have had a hard time, so we need to be kind to them. Tomorrow I will show the father some good places to find food for his family. Safari, you could take the son to meet your friends. He is called Meza."

"Alright, Daddy, but they looked very scary to me standing up and staring."

The next morning, Safari left Tutu in the nest and made his way rather slowly to the nest of the new neighbours. He still wasn't very sure, but his dad had told him there was nothing to be frightened of. When he reached the nest, he saw Meza peeping out from behind his mum. He seemed scared, too, so Safari gave him a big smile and held out a small sweet banana which he had brought from home.

Meza smiled back and jabbered a reply, which Safari tried to understand. He decided it meant "Thank you." Safari then asked if he would like to meet his friends, trying to use his hands to help him understand.

The two boys swung from one tree to the next, Safari leading the way, until they reached the clearing where the monkey children gathered to play. Then Safari jumped down, followed quickly by Meza. The other monkeys were scared and ran away, but Safari shouted to them that his new friend was a mountain monkey and told them the story of their long journey to the forest in order to find food.

"We don't like him," said one of Safari's friends.

"He looks weird," said another.

"Tell him to stop staring at us," said a third, "and tell him to go back to the mountains. We need all the food here. There might not be enough for us if other monkey tribes come here. We don't want him."

Safari was shocked. He thought his friends were being very mean. He was glad that Meza couldn't understand what they had said, but when he looked at his face, he could see that he understood they didn't like him or want him there.

"You are mean and selfish," he shouted to his friends. "If there wasn't any food in the forest and you had to travel for days and days to the mountains, and when you arrived the monkeys there told you to go home, how would you feel?"

"Come Meza," he said slowly to his new friend, "I'll show you my favourite tree and it's full of fruit." He beckoned to Meza and the two monkeys went back into the trees and swung to the mango tree which Safari loved. They picked lots of ripe fruit, eating some, then taking a couple of mangoes back to their families. That was difficult because it was hard to hold a mango and swing from branch to branch, but they managed. They were laughing so much at each other's antics and were best friends by the time they got home. Meza tried to teach Safari how to stand on his back legs, but he fell over so many times and they laughed so much that their mothers came to see what all the noise was about.

That night Safari told his father what had happened and the horrible things his friends had said about Meza.

"I'm afraid that others can be very unkind about strangers just because they look different, talk strangely and have customs we don't understand, but God made them, just as

He made us, and loves all His creatures. We must do the same. I'm proud of you, Safari, that you looked after Meza and I'm sure your friends will soon stop being unkind to him when they see your good example."

Safari thought for a moment. He remembered that he and Tutu had been scared the day before when they had seen a mountain monkey for the first time, but now he knew that he had a very good new friend and they had lots of fun playing together. He hoped his other friends would soon accept him, too.

"I wonder if he can play football?" he thought to himself. "I must ask him tomorrow."

How do you feel when you meet people who have come from another country to live near you? Are you kind to them and make friends with them? Think how you might feel if you had to go to another country and couldn't understand what people were saying?

SAFARI MAKES A CHOICE

It was Saturday, and Safari always loved Saturdays. It was a fun day when he could go and play with his friends, and his favourite game was football.

He got up early and went searching for some sweet bananas, which was his favourite breakfast and one all little monkeys loved. He was gobbling them down when he heard his mother call him. At first, he pretended not to hear, but soon she had swung down from the nest and took his hand, just as he'd finished his last banana.

"Safari, I was calling you – why didn't you listen?" she asked him.

"Sorry, Mum," he answered very sulkily as he wanted to rush away and meet his friends, and he guessed his mum wanted him to help with something.

"Safari, I know that it's Saturday morning and you want to be with your friends, but I need you to take a *very* important message to your Auntie. If you go at once, you will have time to play later."

"Do I have to?" grumbled Safari. "Can't you send Tutu instead. He can manage to swing on the trees now. It's not fair – it's my playday!"

"He's too small and it's too far for him. I need you to go. This message is very important and so I am trusting you to take it safely. Please go now."

His mum had spoken in the sort of voice he knew he had to obey, so he took the message and put it into the pocket in his jacket and started on his way with a big, grumpy sigh.

He was *not* happy. In fact, Safari was *very* cross. He began to make his way through the forest, swinging from tree to tree. But it was such a lovely morning that he just couldn't be cross for long as the sun shone on his back as he swung along through the forest.

When he came to a clearing quite a way from his home, he saw a group of monkeys playing football on the grass. He stopped to watch them. "After all," he said to himself, "I need a little rest".

His feet were itching to join in and one of the monkeys called over to him, "Hi! Come and play with us".

"Sorry, I can't today," he answered.

Safari knew he should have walked away and continued with his important journey, but he chose to watch for a bit longer.

"I bet you don't know how to play football," another monkey taunted him. "I bet you're just a softie and don't know how to play!"

"Of course, I know how to play!" Safari felt himself getting angry, "and what is more, I am *good* at football".

"Come and prove it then," was the reply.

Safari hesitated. He knew he could show those monkeys a thing or two! Can't play indeed! He was fantastic – a star – at football! A little voice inside his head was telling him that it wouldn't matter if he stopped and played for a little while. After all, nobody would know, and he could still take the message to his auntie afterwards. It would be fun to play, and his feet were longing to kick the ball.

Safari started to take off his jacket so that he could play, when he felt the letter inside the pocket - it seemed to burn into his body. He thought of his mum. It must have been very important for her to have asked him to give up his Saturday and visit his auntie. He thought of his auntie, whom he loved very much, and remembered that Mum said she was trusting him to deliver it. He thought hard for a few moments, then made his choice. He buttoned up his jacket again, turned his back on the monkeys in the clearing and walked away shouting, "I'm not playing today, I have to visit my auntie."

"Chicken … chicken … chicken!" they chanted as he ran for the nearest tree and climbed up to swing across the branches. He tried not to let the tears roll down his cheeks as he heard the chanting and taunting of the monkeys, and was glad when he was out of earshot. He went as quickly as he could, arriving out of breath as he ran up the tree where his auntie lived.

Safari's auntie was surprised to see her nephew. She was just going out but stopped to greet him and offered him some bananas and a drink.

"I have a *very* important message from Mum," he told her, taking the letter from his pocket and giving it to her to read. Her face looked shocked as she read it.

"Oh Safari," she exclaimed, "thank goodness you came so quickly with this message. You probably have saved my life! Your mum has learnt about a trap that has been set where I was supposed to be going this morning, and you arrived just in the nick of time! If you had been any later then I would have already gone and been caught in the trap. O thank you, dear, what a good monkey-child you have been!"

Auntie was so pleased that she gave him a special present to reward him for his journey, and guess what it was? It was a new football which she had made for him, with lovely shiny leaves all carefully bound together with twine.

Safari was so pleased – pleased that he didn't stop to play with the monkeys in the forest, but most of all pleased that his auntie had not been hurt or killed in a trap and pleased with his lovely new football.

Safari's auntie decided to accompany him back to his home. As they went along the way she entertained him by telling him lots of stories of what it was like when she was a monkey-child, and Safari felt so happy.

When they arrived back at Safari's home his mother also praised him for obeying her and he was ashamed that he had been so cross when his mum asked him to take a message and then that he almost stopped and played football. Thank goodness he had chosen to obey his mum.

Safari was tempted to stop and play football. If he had done so, his auntie would have been hurt and maybe even killed. It was hard to decide to do the right thing and not to please himself. When we are tempted to do things we know are wrong, we can ask Jesus to help us make the right choice.

SAFARI AND THE HUMAN CHILDREN

Very often Safari would say to his mum that he was bored! Life seemed so ordinary living up in the nest in the trees, eating bananas every day (although they were his favourite food) and he longed for more adventures in the BIG BEYOND - the world beyond his nest.

One day he was sitting up in the nest and thinking. Have you ever thought what monkeys do when they think? They sit and scratch their heads! Thinking of adventures made him forget about some of the scary things which had happened to him when he had gone exploring the BIG BEYOND once before, and he began to jabber and squeak as he thought of a good idea.

Every morning he watched the human children walk down the trail with things on their heads and every afternoon he watched them walk back. They were talking away to each other, but he couldn't understand what they were saying. It wasn't monkey jabber – not even different monkey jabber such as Meza his mountain monkey friend spoke.

His big idea was that he would follow them into the BIG BEYOND and try to become a human child. After all, he had nice clothes, his posh jacket and his hat, so he looked as smart as they did. One morning he decided that this was the day he would follow them. He ran down from the nest as they passed by, keeping a safe distance behind them and hoping he wouldn't be seen. One child did turn around and see him and he quickly scampered up the nearest tree. Safari's mother had always warned her children to be scared of humans in case they caught them and turned them into mincemeat for their food!

When he felt it was safe to do so, he climbed back down the tree and began to follow them again. They all went into a big hut which had a grass roof. "What a big 'nest' they have," Safari thought, scratching his head, because that's what monkeys do when they are thinking.

Rather scared, Safari poked his head around the doorway and watched the children unwrap the parcels of books which they had been carrying on their heads. Then they sat down on benches. Safari wanted to go and sit with them because he so wanted to be a human child, but he was too scared to join them. He had put a parcel under his hat, too, thinking that if he wore clothes like the human children and had a parcel on his head just as they did, it would change him into a human child. In his parcel, though, there was a banana – just in case he felt hungry and needed a snack.

At the front of the hut was a big man, who held a stick in his hand and wrote some things on a big black board on the wall. The teacher began to talk, but he made noises that Safari couldn't understand at all – it wasn't like monkey jabber. He *so* wanted to understand, and he scratched his head *very* hard as he tried to hear what was said and tried to make sense of the marks on the black board – but even though he tried and tried, it was no use. He couldn't understand a thing.

Then a child turned towards the door and saw Safari standing there and screamed. Everyone turned around and stared at

Safari, making him feel very frightened. He scampered away as fast as he could, not looking where he was going, because he had tears in his eyes and was very upset.

Suddenly he bumped into Mukubwa, the big chimpanzee.

"Whatever is the matter, Safari?" he asked him. Tears began to pour from his eyes and he sobbed, "I thought that if I looked like a human child with nice clothes, had a parcel on my head just like they carry, went where they went and did what they did, I would become a human child – but I couldn't understand the marks on the board or what the big human man was saying – and I *so* wanted to be a human child!"

Mukubwa took Safari's little paw into his big one.

"O Safari, that is only monkey wisdom. No matter how hard you try to copy the human children, it will never change you into one! You were born a monkey and you will always be a monkey! The only way to become a human child is to be born as one – and that isn't possible for a monkey. Dry your eyes and eat your banana and run back home." A sadder and wiser Safari did just that.

It is easy for us to think we are Christians because we live in a Christian country. Maybe we dress smartly on Sundays and go to Church and try to copy what Christian people do, but that will *never* make us a Christian. But we have wonderful news – we can be born a second time into God's family and become His children (for that is what Christians are), if we ask Jesus to forgive us for all the bad things we have said and done and ask Him to bring us into God's family. Safari could never become a human child, but we can become God's child, if only we ask Him.

SAFARI'S ADVENTURE WITH HIS FATHER

A little while after Safari recovered from his adventure following the children to school and learning that he could never become a human child, he once again began to get restless and longed for another adventure.

"I'm bored mummy – what can I do?" he often asked. His mum looked at him and told him in monkey jabber to go and play with his friends and little brother, but he wanted something more exciting than that.

Every day he woke up and scratched his head, thinking, "What can I do today? Where can I explore?"

He didn't want to go to the river again, in case he fell in; he didn't want to go to the school again because he wasn't a human child. Then one day he had a great idea! He would follow the male monkeys when they went on their hunting trip deep into the forest, over the hills and far away. It was a brilliant idea and he wondered why he hadn't thought of it before. It would be so cool to have a new adventure, better than playing with little Tutu, even though he loved his brother very much.

Safari knew that he would have to be *very* quiet as he followed them, for the adult male monkeys would be angry if they found a monkey-child was tagging along behind them, uninvited. A monkey had to be almost grown up to be invited on such a trip.

So, Safari waited quietly at the edge of the forest as the fathers set off. Then he began to follow them, swinging from branch to branch, just close enough to see them, but far enough away for him not to be heard. He tried not to make one jabber or squeak in case he gave the game away. It was difficult to keep the hunters in his sight because they had much longer arms than his and they swung quickly through the trees until they reached the tree they were searching for, which was full of juicy berries.

Safari's mouth watered at the sight of them, as the adults picked and ate them, jabbering in their excitement. He had to keep himself hidden in case he was discovered, but by the time they had finished gathering the berries and moved on, he was very hungry and he saw that there were no berries left! In his haste to follow the adults that morning, Safari had even forgotten to bring a banana as a snack! A big tear began to roll down his cheek, but he wiped it away. He was hungry, tired and a long way from home! All this sadness made him lose his balance and he fell from the tree with a huge squeak of fear, into the undergrowth beneath him.

The male monkeys looked around when they heard the noise, and they looked angry and fierce! Safari was even more scared. What would they do to him?

Then a big monkey paw patted him and picked him up. Safari closed his eyes, too scared to look.

"Safari, it's you! I might have known it – you are too adventurous for your own good!"

Safari knew that voice – it was his dad!

"Come on, I'll carry you home. Why didn't you ask me to take you, not follow on your own?"

Safari was so glad to hear his dad's voice and have his big, strong arms around him, and he cuddled him all the way home.

Our Father, God, knows each one of us by our name. When we try to do 'our own thing' we soon get into trouble. We can ask Jesus to be with us and help us and keep us safe every day.

SAFARI HAS AN ADVENTURE IN THE BIG BEYOND

A little while after Safari had followed the adults into the forest, he did have a very special adventure.

He woke up one morning to find his father shaking him gently.

"Safari, get up. You are coming with me today."

Safari felt very excited and proud to think that his dad was going to take him out. He brushed down his jacket and straightened up his hat, then remembered to grab a couple of sweet bananas, and was ready to set off.

"Where are we going, Daddy?" he asked.

"Oh, don't worry about that. It's quite a long and difficult way, but you'll be ok as I'm here to look after you. All you need to worry about is that you stay close to me. Don't wander off in the forest or you might get lost."

"But I *want* to know where we are going," persisted Safari. "Is it to the mountains, or deep into the forest? Please, where are we going?"

Daddy smiled at the little monkey. "It's no use keeping on my son, because I'm not going to tell you. You just need to know that you must keep close to me and you will be safe. I will look after you."

Safari and his dad set off in the direction of the river. Before long they arrived at the river-bank, and, as you know, most forest monkeys don't like water. Safari could see things which looked like floating logs, but every now and then one would move suddenly, and he realised they were hungry crocodiles! Safari held on to his daddy's paw *very* tightly.

"We are going to cross the river now," his dad told him. Cross the river! Oh no! Safari began to tremble he was so scared. He looked at the crocodiles and thought that even his dad couldn't save him from being eaten by them.

Dad looked at him and smiled. "Trust me, little Safari," he said. "Would I let you get hurt or allow a crocodile to eat you?"

He swung Safari onto his back and reminded him to hold on tightly and trust him. Then Dad ran up a big tree and began to swing from one branch to another, and from one tree to another. With one last huge jump, they were safely over the river and on the other bank.

"That wasn't too bad, was it?" asked Dad.

"No, I felt quite safe on your back and it was fun swinging through the trees."

They continued their journey, climbing some steep rocks on the other side. Safari's legs were a bit tired and he let go of his dad's paw so that he could use both hands to scramble over the rocks. Soon he began to fall behind and almost lost sight of his father. He began to jabber and grumble under his breath, just loud enough that his dad could hear a noise, but quiet enough that he couldn't hear the actual words.

"It's hot and I'm tired. What's Daddy doing, bringing me out here – it's not fair, he hasn't even looked back to see where

I am." Safari was beginning to feel sorry for himself and wasn't so sure that coming out with his father was such a good idea after all.

Suddenly Safari heard a hiss – and there, staring him in the face was a huge snake, looking for all the world that it was going to strike him. The little monkey froze with fear, too scared for a moment even to scream. Inside his head he was silently crying out, "Daddy, Daddy, where are you?"

Of course, his daddy was looking after him and knew exactly where Safari was. He hadn't let him out of his sight for one second, but he also knew that Safari had to learn to obey and keep close to him at all times, so he had allowed him to think that his daddy wasn't watching or caring.

Before the snake could lash out, Daddy's long arm had picked him up and put him on his back.

Safari pestered his father to know where they were going. If he had told his son all about the journey, he might have become discouraged and given up before they had started.

We sometimes want God to tell us about the way ahead, but Father God knows that we might become discouraged and He wants us to trust Him.

THE JOURNEY CONTINUES

For quite a long way Safari was content to stay and rest on his daddy's back, and it was a long time before he stopped shaking with fear. They travelled together in this way up the mountain until they found a nice place for a picnic, where they sat down and ate sweet bananas, then played football together using a mango which had fallen from a tree. It was fun and Safari felt so much better that he forgot all about the horrible crocodiles and the snake he had seen earlier in the day. Soon it was time to go on with the journey.

"Are we nearly there?" he asked.

"Not quite," was the answer, "but don't worry. When you get tired, tell me, and you can ride on my back. Don't be afraid, I'm your father and will always look after you. All you have to remember is to stay close to me."

The path led them into the big forest. There were lots of interesting things to see and Safari was excited. He kept darting off to look at things or follow a scent that was interesting, but always kept his father in his sight. After a while Safari became bolder and started to go down some of the side paths, scampering away from his dad. He wandered down a particularly interesting one because he could smell the scent of ripe fruit and thought a snack would be a nice thing to have.

Suddenly, a twig cracked, and he fell into a large hole in the ground – it was a trap!

He screamed with fear, but the scream just seemed to echo around the dark hole. His foot hurt, so even when he tried to get out, he couldn't do so. He began to feel cold, lonely and afraid.

Tears began to roll down his face. "O why didn't I obey Dad and keep close to him?" he thought to himself, scratching his head in despair. "I might be lost forever in this dark hole, or a lion might come and eat me." Safari listened hoping against hope that he might hear his dad swinging through the trees to find him. Then he realised that his daddy could be a long way down the trail by now and not know which path his son had taken.

He heard the noises of the forest and they all seemed very scary to Safari. Then there was a *very* loud noise – something *very* large was coming his way and he hid as far back in the hole as he could.

The noise stopped and a big grey 'thing' appeared and lifted the top of the trap away. The grey 'thing' pulled out the terrified monkey and swished him up high, right into his father's arms. Tembo the elephant had rescued him! His father was sitting on the elephant's back, and Safari snuggled into arms, crying, "Sorry, sorry, sorry."

His father just cuddled him and stroked his head – glad he had been rescued and wasn't badly hurt.

Tembo continued to take them both through the forest and into a beautiful place which took Safari's breath away. There were rocks and trees, grass and flowers, and monkeys chasing around and playing, and masses of food for them to eat.

"Here we are, Safari, safe and sound," announced his dad, as Tembo swung them down using his strong trunk.

"I want you to meet lots of your relatives, who have gathered here to have a party for you."

"Today," his dad continued, "you have learnt to trust me that I will take care of you and also that whatever you do, even if you go off on your own way and get into trouble, I still love you and will take care of you. That is a *big lesson* for a small monkey to learn. Now have fun and enjoy the party I have arranged for you."

Safari did have fun; but he also never forgot the lesson about trusting his father and obeying him.

We can be just like Safari and forget to stay close to our Father God, who loves us so much and longs to keep us safe. Can you think of ways which help you to stay close to God?